My 1st Classic Story

DANIEL BOONE

a retelling by Eric Blair

illustrated by Micah Chambers-Goldberg

PICTURE WINDOW BOOKS

a capstone imprint

My First Classic Story is published by Picture Window Books

A Capstone Imprint

151 Good Counsel Drive, P.O. Box 669

Mankato, Minnesota 56002

www.capstonepub.com

Printed in the United States of America in Stevens Point, Wisconsin.

092010

005934WZS11

Library of Congress Cataloging-in-Publication Data

Blair, Eric.

Daniel Boone / retold by Eric Blair ; illustrated by Micah Chambers-Goldberg.

p. cm. — (My first classic story)

ISBN 978-1-4048-6578-5 (library binding)

1. Boone, Daniel, 1734-1820—Juvenile literature. 2. Pioneers—Kentucky—
Biography—Juvenile literature. 3. Frontier and pioneer life—Kentucky—
Juvenile literature. 4. Kentucky—Biography—Juvenile literature.
I. Chambers-Goldberg, Micah, ill. II. Title.

F454.B66B56 2011

976.9'02092—dc22

[B]   2010030646

Art Director: Kay Fraser

Graphic Designer: Emily Harris

Production Specialist: Michelle Biedscheid

For generations, storytelling was the main form of entertainment. Some of the greatest stories were tall tales, or exaggerated stories that may or may not have been about real people.

Daniel Boone was born in 1734 in a log cabin in Pennsylvania. He became a true American pioneer and one of the first folk heroes in the United States.

Daniel Boone was a born hunter.
One day, Daniel threw a diaper pin across
the room.

It hit his bottle! His parents knew that he would be a great hunter.

To be a good hunter, Daniel needed many skills.

Indians taught Daniel how to hunt.

Daniel learned to track and trap wild animals. He also learned to fish.

Daniel hunted deer, bears, and birds for his family to eat.

Daniel hunted with knives and tomahawks.

He could throw them farther than other
men could see.

As Daniel grew, his adventures grew. Once,
he wrestled with a huge grizzly bear for
three days.

On the third day, the bear gave up and
went back to its cave.

Daniel's older brother made him a long rifle.

With his new rifle, Daniel could shoot a tick off a deer.

He could shoot an acorn out of a tree.

19

Daniel decided to move to the West.

There were no easy roads to get there.
Daniel followed the trail of the Indians
and buffalo.

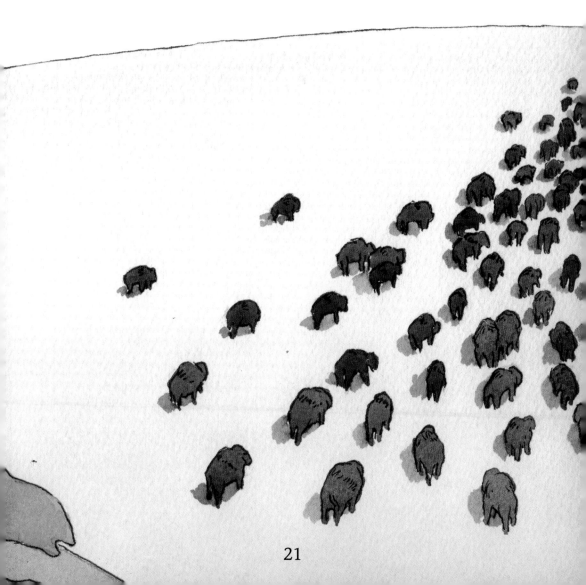

Daniel wanted other people to move west, too.

He got fifteen men with axes.
Together, they cleared the trail for more
settlers.

Soon, people were headed west on
Daniel Boone's Wilderness Road.

The road wasn't always safe. Sometimes, Daniel would hide in the trees to protect the people.

He would shoot at bears and bandits to scare them away.

One day, Daniel saw two blue eyes in the forest. He'd never seen an animal with blue eyes.

The eyes belonged to a girl named Rebecca.
She loved the wild as much as Daniel did.

Daniel and Rebecca decided to get married.

They built a log cabin in the West and
lived happily ever after.

The End